SLIP STREAM

OOTBALL LEGEND

DAVID AND **HELEN ORME**
Illustrated by **ROB HEASLEY**

978 1 4451 1812 3 pb

978 1 4451 1811 6 pb

978 1 4451 1813 0 pb

hic fiction

978 1 4451 1799 7 pb

978 1 4451 1801 7 pb

978 1 4451 1800 0 pb

-fiction

SLIP STREAM

FOOTBALL LEGEND

DAVID AND **HELEN ORME**
Illustrated by **ROB HEASLEY**

EDGE
FRANKLIN WATTS

LONDON • SYDNEY

First published in 2013 by
Franklin Watts
338 Euston Road
London NW1 3BH

Franklin Watts Australia
Level 17/207 Kent Street
Sydney NSW 2000

Text © David and Helen Orme 2013
Illustration © Franklin Watts 2013

The rights of David and Helen Orme to be
identified as the authors and Rob Heasley
as the illustrator of this Work have been
asserted in accordance with the Copyright,
Designs and Patents Act, 1988.

A CIP catalogue record for this book is
available from the British Library.

ISBN 978 1 4451 1811 6

Series Editors: Adrian Cole and Jackie Hamley
Series Advisors: Diana Bentley and Dee Reid
Series Designer: Peter Scoulding

1 3 5 7 9 10 8 6 4 2

Printed in China

Franklin Watts is a division of
Hachette Children's Books,
an Hachette UK company.
www.hachette.co.uk

CONTENTS

CHAPTER 1
WIMP BOY!

"Coming to play football?" asked Phil.

"No," said Rob. "I'm going to see my granddad."

"Wimp boy!" sneered Martin. He shoved Rob hard against the wall. "You won't make the team if you just hang around with some old bloke! In fact, I'll see to it that you don't."

"Back off," said Phil. "You're always on his case."

Rob said nothing. He knew Martin wouldn't believe him about his granddad.

The trials for the school football team were on Monday. Rob hoped that he would make the team. And that Martin wouldn't.

CHAPTER 2
OLD BLOKE

Rob's granddad was in the garden when Rob arrived.

Granddad was wearing his England shirt. It was very

special to him.

"OK Rob," said Granddad. "Dribble round the cones

then shoot. Control it!"

Rob made a great job of the dribbling, but his shot

was too wide.

"Use the inside of your foot more," said Granddad.

"Like this!"

Granddad's shot powered like a bullet. It went straight through the posts and over the fence.

"Argh!" came a cry.

Out staggered Martin!

He had been hiding by the fence to spy on Rob.

Granddad's shot had hit him smack in the face.

CHAPTER 3

FOOTBALL LEGEND

Just then, Phil came round the corner.

He took one look at Rob's granddad.

"Wow!" he said. "You're Bobby James!

You used to play for England!"

Then Phil turned to Rob.

"You should have told us your granddad

was a football legend!"

"Nice to be recognised!" said Granddad.

"Why don't you join us for a kickabout?"

Martin said nothing.

He was too busy trying not to cry.

CHAPTER 4
FOOTBALL TRIALS

On Monday, Rob and Phil had their trial.

Martin couldn't play.

His eye was still too swollen.

In the first half, Rob scored one goal.

In the second half, Phil hit the cross bar.

After the match, the team coach smiled at Rob

and Phil. "You were brilliant, lads!" he said.

Then Granddad called them over. "Rob! Phil!

I'd like you to meet an old friend. He's a

talent scout now..."

Rob and Phil hurried over.

Martin stared at them.

"Shame you didn't get a chance to show off

your talent," said Rob.

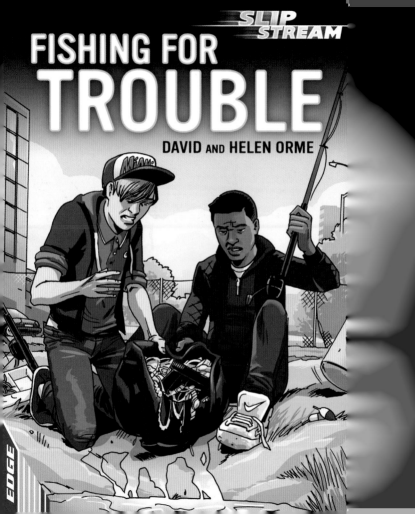

Will and Adam go fishing every weekend.
It keeps them away from the gangs on their estate.

Then, one day, they catch more
than they bargained for.

How will they keep out of trouble now?

EDGE
FRANKLIN WATTS

LONDON•SYDNEY

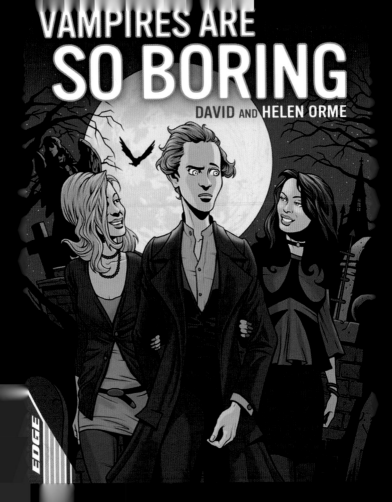

VAMPIRES ARE
SO BORING

DAVID AND HELEN ORME

In a lonely churchyard, a vampire wakes.
He must find food... human blood.

Two girls find him – they want him to be their
boyfriend like the vampire off the telly.
But the vampire has other ideas...

LONDON·SYDNEY

FOR TEACHERS

About SLIP STREAM

Slipstream is a series of expertly levelled books designed for pupils who are struggling with reading. Its unique three-strand approach through fiction, graphic fiction and non-fiction gives pupils a rich reading experience that will accelerate their progress and close the reading gap.

At the heart of every Slipstream fiction book is a great story. Easily accessible words and phrases ensure that pupils both decode and comprehend, and the high interest stories really engage older struggling readers.

Whether you're using Slipstream Level 2 for Guided Reading or as an independent read, here are some suggestions:

1. Make each reading session successful. Talk about the text before the pupil starts reading. Introduce any unfamiliar vocabulary.

2. Encourage the pupil to talk about the book using a range of open questions. For example, what would be their dream job?

3. Discuss the differences between reading fiction, graphic fiction and non-fiction. What do they prefer?

Slipstream Level 2 photocopiable **WORKBOOK** ISBN: 978 1 4451 1797 3 available – download free sample worksheets from: www.franklinwatts.co.uk

For guidance, SLIPSTREAM Level 2 – Football Legend has been approximately measured to:

National Curriculum Level: 2b
Reading Age: 7.6–8.0
Book Band: Purple

ATOS: 2.1*
Guided Reading Level: I
Lexile® Measure (confirmed): 350L

*Please check actual Accelerated Reader™ book level and quiz availability at www.arbookfind.co.uk